WARRIOR OF LIGHT

ROBERT DALE

WARRIOR OF LIGHT
Copyright © 2024 by Robert Dale

Scripture quotations marked KJV are taken from the Holy Bible, King James Version, which is in the public domain.

ISBN: 978-1-4866-2600-7
eBook ISBN: 978-1-4866-2601-4

Word Alive Press
119 De Baets Street Winnipeg, MB R2J 3R9
www.wordalivepress.ca

WORD ALIVE
—P R E S S—

Cataloguing in Publication information can be obtained from Library and Archives Canada.

To my brother Chris:
I told you I'd be great with a sword!

Put on the whole armour of God, that ye may be able to stand against the wiles of the devil. For we wrestle not against flesh and blood, but against principalities, against powers, against the rulers of the darkness of this world, against spiritual wickedness in high places. Wherefore take unto you the whole armour of God, that ye may be able to withstand in the evil day, and having done all, to stand. Stand therefore, having your loins girt about with truth, and having on the breastplate of righteousness; and your feet shod with the preparation of the gospel of peace; above all, taking the shield of faith, wherewith ye shall be able to quench all the fiery darts of the wicked. And take the helmet of salvation, and the sword of the Spirit, which is the word of God. (Ephesians 6:11–17)

ONE

I t was a beautiful, warm summer night in a rural field. Thousands of crickets chirped endlessly as a bright moon in the black sky accentuated by countless stars lit the landscape. An unkept laneway at the edge of the field contained a lone vehicle with a lone occupant. The vehicle was a well-used pickup truck, and it was enveloped in a thicker blackness than the night around it. This blackness was even more heavily surrounding the youngish man inside of the truck, and the natural beauty of the area was lost on him. He had more serious things on his mind. Much more serious.

He held two objects, one in his right hand and one in his left, and was greatly struggling with which he should choose. His left held his cell phone, while his right held a pistol! He didn't know which felt heavier.

A broken man, he felt he couldn't take any more of what life had dealt him, and he was looking for something more. He made one last desperate vocal plea.

"Oh God, if you're there and Nancy was right that you care and love me, *please show me!*"

The silence that followed erased the last of his hope.

"I guess I know what I have to do then," he blurted out as tears streamed down his face.

Flipping the safety switch on the gun, he began to raise it to his head.

Suddenly the cab was brightly lit by a white glow, which caused him to pause and made that enveloping darkness retreat. Realizing it was coming from the cell phone, he looked at the screen and saw one word—DON'T!

Bewildered by this unexpected message, he clicked the safety back on the weapon and set it down.

Staring at the screen, he suddenly realized that the phone was ringing!

"Hello?" he said, answering it.

"Oh nuts!" an older male voice responded. "I was trying to phone my wife."

A light whimper and a dejected sigh escaped the younger man as the darkness threatened again.

"Okay, sorry," was all that could exit his mouth, and with that, he hung up.

The previous inky blackness began to settle over him again.

Lifting the firearm once more, he repeated the motion of releasing the safety and raising it. He felt the need to vocalize his great disappointment once more as he stated, "That proves it. He doesn't exist, or if He does, He doesn't care."

The bright light returned with what seemed like even more intensity. Its brightness shocked him again as the message on the phone repeated: DON'T.

"Hello?"

"Hey, young man, it's me again." The same old man's voice.

"Ok, wrong number again?" A sniffled query.

"No, I think from the sound of your voice you need someone to talk to, and I'm offering to listen."

What? Why would this old guy wanna hear what he had to say?

"Why?" he asked incredulously.

"As I said, I'm willing to listen, and I believe God wants me to meet with you."

God? Was this an actual response from Him? He began to hope a tiny bit, and the black fog began to recede from his mind.

A whisper seemed to say, "Go."

A hesitant yet hopeful response came. "Ok, where do you want to meet?" He couldn't believe he was actually entertaining the idea.

"You know the coffee shop on the corner of First and Main?"

"Yeah, Murphy's"

"That's the one. What's your name, by the way?"

"Ben."

"Ok, Ben, I'm Harold, but you can call me Harry if you like. Anyway, I'll be at Murphy's in ten minutes. Sound good?"

"Sure, see you then." A glimmer of hope began in him as he started the pickup and drove down the road back into town.

The menacing blackness followed.

TWO

urphy's was a twenty-four-hour restaurant and coffee shop where many truckers and overnight workers stopped for a coffee or warm meal.

The food was good, and the staff were friendly. There was almost always someone to talk to, if you wanted. After driving back from the outskirts of town, down the streets he knew all too well, the restaurant came into view. He pulled up outside of it and then got out of the pickup and walked inside, wondering how he would recognize this Harold.

He needn't have worried.

"Ben?" The question came from a tall, thin, well-aged man who Ben guessed was in his seventies, standing just inside the entrance.

"Harold." A polite nod toward the question and an awkwardly extended hand.

"I'm glad you showed up; let's sit and have a coffee, shall we?" the older man invited with a warm smile.

They sat in a booth well away from the other occupants of the establishment for some privacy.

After the coffee arrived, Harold looked seriously, yet kindly, at the younger man.

"So where would you like to start?" he queried.

A deep, much calmer breath than he imagined possible with what had almost happened just a short while ago gave him the courage to begin. "I don't quite know what to say. It's difficult to talk about, and I don't really know you." A feeble attempt but a start nonetheless.

The darkness was trying to settle in on his mind once again.

A small, light chuckle escaped the older man. "I understand that, believe me I do, but the beginning of great friendships is always between strangers."

"Yes … yes, I guess it is." *Wow, pretty smart, this old guy*, Ben thought. *Maybe I should be careful.*

That blackness again.

"I see the struggle to trust me with what's on your mind, but you've come down here to meet, so why not go the full distance?" The question came from the mouth of Harold, but Ben felt within himself that same argument.

"Ok." A wary glance around them, making sure no one else could hear. "I'll try to explain what happened tonight, but the point is I almost … ended it." Shame caused him to bow his head and avoid the other's eyes.

"I thought it might be something close to that. May I ask why?"

Ben looked up at the question. Gentle was the tone, and kindness was what he saw in the face of his coffee partner.

"That's the hard part. I've been struggling so much with what happened, telling is much more difficult."

"Do you mind if I say a short prayer?" The question surprised the younger man, as did his desire for the prayer.

"Yes, please."

"Father, please help Ben with what he's trying to share with me. You know what has happened in his life and how much he's struggling. Please show him your love for him and give me understanding toward him. In Jesus' name. Amen."

As Ben opened his eyes and lifted his head, he felt the darkness had receded again and that strange light seemed almost to emanate from the older man. Grasping an opening, he began to explain the night's events.

"As I said, I almost ended things tonight, but just as I was about to, I asked God to show me that He cared. That's when you called, and the weirdest thing was, I saw the word 'Don't' on my phone, and a bright light lit up the cab of my truck."

Another small chuckle and glow came from Harold. It felt disrespectful to Ben, and he was about to get angry with Harold when the older man said, "Let me see your phone."

Ben took his cell out of his pocket and opened the recent call list. There was the name D. Ontager as the last two calls in his phone.

DON'T …

THREE

He couldn't believe it! What seemed like a message was simply his misreading the name of who was calling! The blackness came on heavy at this point, and Harold seemed to sense this.

"Don't think this was a mistake, because I assure you it wasn't. I just wanted to show you how God works sometimes."

The light was pushing back against the darkness. This was not a simple struggle. This was a major battle.

"How? By making me think He cares when it's just my own error?"

"Do you really think I dialed a number I've never known?"

The aged man brought his own cell phone out and showed Ben the call history. Two calls showed as the last dialed to the same number: "Home."

What ... how? Ben's mind fought to comprehend what he was looking at.

"God surely does care. This was His doing; He didn't want your life to end tonight. So tell me what led you to this point, Ben."

A further kind look and brightness clearing the dense fog caused the young man to open up. "I lost my wife and unborn child. They were killed two years ago in a car crash." A tear and a quivering lip were all that followed the statement.

The older man had tears in his own eyes as he proclaimed: "Thank you, Father, I now finally understand. Praise you for showing me why!"

Ben couldn't understand, but he didn't have to wait long for an explanation. Harold held up a hand to signal Ben to wait.

"When I was twenty-four years old, I was in love with a beautiful young woman who became my wife and soon was pregnant with our first child." A quick, painful inhale and he went on. "She was killed on the job during her last week of work before her maternity leave. I lost both of them. I now finally know why that happened, finally, almost fifty years later!"

Shock ran through the young man's mind. How could it be that this man had experienced the same thing so long ago and hadn't lost his mind completely as Ben almost had?

"Believe me, Ben, it was no picnic recovering from that experience. My life changed dramatically after that point, and it was actually that event that brought me to the Lord."

The brightness felt so intense now, Ben couldn't believe that it wasn't visual.

"So you believe God allowed you to lose your wife and child that long ago so I could talk to you about losing my own family this many years later?" The question was asked with incredulity.

"Completely. Was your wife a believer in Jesus?"

"Yes."

"So was mine, but I wasn't, not then. That came later."

"Why, though? Why would God allow such a huge amount of pain just to get you to find Him? There must have been another way!"

Dark and light were battling hard now.

"There wasn't. I know that now. I wasn't interested in going to the services that my wife attended. I didn't read the Bible at all or even make an attempt at praying. My life was my own. I did what I wanted when I wanted, and no one, not even God, could tell me otherwise." The wrinkled face looked at Ben with what seemed to be the question of "Sound familiar?"

It did. Very familiar.

FOUR

ore people were beginning to fill up the restaurant, as a shift change had just happened in many of the local warehouses and factories. Ben was getting uncomfortable talking about this with so many able to hear. Rising from the table, he stated, "I need a smoke."

"You go ahead. I need to call my wife for a minute, but we need to talk some more."

Ben went to his truck and lit a cigarette. His mind was reeling with all that had happened, and he knew that this was the most important crossroads in his life that he had ever faced.

The light was pushing hard against the darkness now.

Things were becoming clearer to Ben than they had ever been, but he still had questions. As he dragged on the cigarette, he reflected on the events of his life. Nancy had, in different ways, said the same kind of things Harold was saying. Why hadn't he listened? He knew the answer even as his mind asked the question.

"Because I didn't want to." He spoke it aloud.

"Do you want to now?" Harold asked as he walked toward Ben.

"I think I have to." The young man had a desperate look, one that Harold knew all too well.

"I just told Doreen, my wife, that I'd be a little longer. Let's go to the church building where I attend. It's not far, if you want to follow me," he suggested.

The conflict inside Ben was reaching epic battle proportions. He made a choice.

"Ok, what are you driving?"

The older man pointed out his car and they began the short drive.

They arrived at the church in just a few minutes. Harold was right—it wasn't far and was easy to find. The older man had two more coffees and a small bag with him. As they walked to the door, he handed them to Ben.

"Thought we could use these. Apple fritters—don't tell Doreen!" A small smile came with the admonishment. He proceeded to unlock and swing the door wide. Entering the establishment, he flipped a few lights on and led Ben to the main auditorium. There was a small table set around the corner inside the main room. Harold sat at this table and invited the younger man to take a seat.

Ben sat and took a sip from the fresh coffee. Setting the cup down, he looked at the other man and said, "What comes next?"

"You need to decide if you're going to accept Jesus as your own Lord and Saviour. Are you ready to let go and let God?"

The power of the invisible light in this place was so powerful, Ben felt like he could almost see it. It was the opposite to what he had felt earlier with the gun in his hand, and he wanted this new feeling to be permanent in his life.

"Yes, I'm ready. Tell me what to say!"

"Just say it in your own words. Tell Jesus that you know you're a sinner in need of Him. Ask Him to be your Lord and Saviour and tell Him you believe in Him."

Ben bowed his head; he had never been more ready to say these words. "Jesus, I know you've been chasing me all of my life. I know that I've run hard from you and made a mess of my life. Now that Nancy and our child are with you, I want to know you too. Please be my Lord and Saviour. I believe, Oh Lord. Help me with the part that resists you. Save me, I pray, from myself."

Tears streamed down the man's face as he set aside his pride and asked for salvation. A warmth began to fill his chest, and peace washed over him that he had never felt before.

Opening his eyes, he looked down and saw a breastplate where his shirt had been! Startled, he looked up at the other man and saw not a senior but a warrior of old, dressed in full armour, with a shield and helmet emanating the same glow he had felt earlier!

FIVE

As Ben tried to grasp what he was seeing, the warrior spoke.

"Welcome to the family." Harold's voice came from this formidable soldier in front of him!

"Harold?"

"Yes, this is how I look in the spiritual realm," came the reply.

"Spiritual realm?" A seed of understanding began to grow in his mind. "The darkness I felt is real then?"

"Yes, just as the light that fights against it is. I saw how hard the darkness was trying to keep you from the light. I knew it was your time to be born spiritually, if you were willing."

Ben took a closer look at this person before him. He saw what appeared to be a senior soldier not unlike a centurion of old. The man was clad in full golden armour, breastplate, belt, greaves, and shoes, even a helmet and very large shield! Strapped to his side was a very capable looking sword, resplendent in its beauty.

"Have a look in the mirror," the warrior advised.

Getting up from the chair, he walked to a mirror that seemed to be mounted on the wall for just such an occasion. What he saw looked similar to the senior soldier with him. He was dressed in a full set of golden armour with the same resplendent sword strapped to his side. That now familiar glow was also emitting from him! The only difference he could see was that his shield was much smaller than the older man's.

"Why is my shield so much smaller than yours?" he asked curiously.

"It is the shield of faith, and as your faith grows, so will the size of your shield."

"So will I only see the world this way now?"

A light chuckle preceded the answer.

"No, you need to focus on which part of reality you want to see. It gets easier with practice."

"Ok, how do I see the physical again?"

"I find food and drink the easiest way to refocus on the physical realm. Focus on the coffee and donuts and let that come into full view."

He realized he was a little hungry now and thought of the apple fritter that was waiting for him. Suddenly the brightness faded and he was seeing Harold sitting at the table with the coffee and bag of donuts at hand.

"Good, that was faster than I expected, but sometimes it will be harder to switch between realms."

The older man opened the bag and handed him a pastry from inside.

"Eat. Switching between realms has a funny effect; it makes the body hungry."

"Why is that?"

"Dunno. It's just my experience with it, never knew why."

"So how do I focus on the spiritual realm to see that side of life?"

"I focus on the Lord; during prayer is a good way as well."

The Lord—his Lord now! Ben felt such joy overwhelm him, and suddenly he was in that spiritual realm again.

"Wow, this is—"

"Too hard to describe really, isn't it?"

"Yeah, it's amazing."

"Ok, come back to the physical. You need to eat and drink, and we have much to discuss."

Another focus on the food and drink brought him back to the physical realm. He finished the snack ravenously and sipped on the coffee afterwards.

"Now you need a Bible of your own. Remember the sword strapped to your side?"

He nodded.

"That's the sword of the Spirit, the Word of God. It's what we use to fight against the darkness."

A Bible—he'd have to read it as much as he could now. The strangest desire came to him now. He wanted to read it! He'd never felt this desire before. It was always the opposite, and he was blissful to experience this change.

Harold handed him a black, leather-bound Bible, typical of what he had seen others carry into church with them, back when he had gone to church with Nancy.

"The church always has a few extras for anyone who needs one. This one is yours now. I suggest you start reading the Gospel of John first."

"Ok, and then?" Eager curiosity filled the new Christian's face.

"Maybe begin at Matthew and read all of the New Testament. Or you could continue on into the book of Acts when you finish John. I'm sorry, at this point I must get home; it's getting late, and Doreen will begin to worry."

Ben suddenly realized how long he had spent with the older man, yet there was so much more that he wanted to learn!

"When can we meet again? I really want to understand more about this new life I've found."

Harold again chuckled lightly.

"It's great to see you so eager. When is your next day off?"

"Friday. I took the night off because I couldn't handle things tonight so well." A bowed head and ashamed look followed the admittance.

"I think the Lord would say taking a night off to find Him is a good reason. Okay, I'll let Doreen know to expect you for supper. Does 6:00 work for you?"

The younger man nodded in acceptance. "Yes please, I'll be there."

They parted ways then, Harold locking up the building again and turning to wave goodbye.

Ben had another cigarette while he waited to make sure the older man was safely on his way. Harold rolled up beside him and put the passenger window down.

"One last thing," the senior soldier advised. "For now, don't switch into the spiritual view while driving; it's tough to focus on driving while doing so." With that admonition, he turned out of the parking lot and drove down the road.

Getting back into his truck, Ben felt the desire to pray again.

"Jesus, Lord, I know you know that I'm new at this, but I want to talk with you and thank you for what has happened. I'm so sorry that I waited so long, but I want to learn from you now and grow in faith in you, please. In Jesus' name. Amen."

Opening his eyes, he realized his focus was set to spiritual, and he could see what Harold meant about driving. He thought about another coffee, and this quickly reset his focus to physical things.

When he got back home, he made himself another coffee, since he normally would be working until 5:30. Opening the brand-new Bible, he saw that it was indexed and separated between the Old and New Testaments. Beginning at the New Testament, he found the Gospel of John. It was the fourth book, and the page number was listed where it could be found. Quickly turning to it, he began to read and realized he had heard a lot of this before.

Memories of his wife reading aloud to herself came to him. *I wish I had listened then*, he berated himself. *Maybe she'd still be here if I had!* He began to feel that old despondency creeping in, and looking up from the scripture, he saw that his focus had shifted to spiritual again. He noticed that the Bible was glowing with pure light yet was still legible. He also noticed a smoke-like dark entity-thing wafting about him! He comprehended that this was a part of the darkness he had felt and talked to Harold about.

"Go away!" He forcefully spoke and saw the smoke dissipate quickly. Feeling no longer the depression of earlier, he continued to read. The joy he began feeling was incredible; he didn't think he could remember a happier time in his life!

SIX

Thursday's shift was about to begin at the warehouse where he worked. Ben was still happy as he walked into the building, but he also was apprehensive about one co-worker—Kranti. This man had been a thorn in his side for many years, and they had nicknamed him "Cranky Kranti." He was from a South Asian country and had told Ben many times that "You Westerners live wrong." He also had a habit of yelling across the warehouse dock at the other workers, demanding that they meet his needs. Many of the others from his country also had a strong dislike for the man, and there had been several complaints to the human resource department about him. Still, Kranti had somehow managed to retain his job with little more than a slap on the wrist.

Ben decided to quickly get to the pre-shift meeting and try to put aside the ill feelings. The night was busy, with overtime available to the afternoon shift, and most chose to stay as long as they could. Receiving was Ben's position, and he was good at it, but tonight was difficult. The loads going out were still cluttering the dock, leaving little room for the inbound trailers to be unloaded. Kranti was his usual unpleasant self, barking orders at anyone he could to help him out. On the last coffee break of the night, he walked up to Ben, who was sitting in his pickup reading this new Bible.

"What are you reading that for? You think you can find God?" A mocking question for sure; he was rarely any other way.

Ben hesitated, afraid of what else Kranti would say.

"I'm a Christian now, and I want to learn more about Jesus." Ben felt a slight redness in his face but also a little pride in stating this.

The response was very surprising to him.

"Good, you need God in your life. I'm happy for you." With that, the usually unpleasant man departed. Shifting into spiritual focus, Ben looked at the withdrawing man and saw that the darkness was thick about him. Ben witnessed something else. Hanging on Kranti's back were several beings of pure blackness! This shocked Ben heavily, but he also recognized the significance of these beings—these demonic things had influenced Ben into almost taking his own life! The rest of the shift went without incident, and Ben found himself on his way home for the weekend.

SEVEN

A rising from sleep in the early afternoon, Ben began to look forward to his upcoming dinner with Harold and his wife. He turned on his stereo, as was his usual custom, and started cleaning his home, since he had a few hours to kill. As the classic rock filled the room, he felt its influence on him; it almost always calmed him in the past when he was having a dark day.

Feeling the familiar soothing feeling, he sang along as decades-old songs wafted from the speakers and filled his mind and emotions. His home had been greatly neglected for a long time, and he felt very ashamed of himself for letting it get to this state. He spent the next two hours clearing tables and counters, throwing out bags of garbage, and filling and running the dishwasher. Looking over his work, he felt a minor sense of accomplishment and knew it was time for a shower so he'd be ready for his upcoming dinner date.

He arrived on time at the address Harold had given him two nights earlier and pulled into a small, single-lane driveway. Getting out of his truck, he took a quick survey of the house. It was a small bungalow-style home set on a single wide lot. There was no garage, and he could see past the house deep into the back yard, which had a medium sized vegetable garden. Two well-worn concrete steps on his left led from the slab pathway beside the drive up to an equally worn concrete landing, and a turn to his right took him up two more steps to the front door. He didn't get the chance to ring the doorbell. The heavy wooden door opened, and Harold greeted him with a welcoming smile, holding the door wide.

"Hello, Ben, won't you come in, please?" the older man invited warmly.

"Thank you, Harold." He stepped through the doorway into a very small vestibule for coats and shoes, which he quickly removed and stored away for later. Looking up from discarding his footwear, he saw a pleasant older lady approach.

"Hello, you must be Ben. I'm Doreen." Her voice sounded like a woman her age, but it was also very welcoming. *Just what you would expect a grandmother's voice should be*, Ben thought to himself. "Please, come in," she continued. "Supper is almost ready. I hope you like pork chops and rice."

Ben admitted that he did as he stepped into the living area of the home. She smiled pleasantly and retreated to the kitchen to check on the meal's progression. While he walked into the room, he began to hum one of the songs from earlier that day.

"I remember that one," Harold commented and named the song.

"Yes, I love the band," Ben openly revealed.

"Our grandson used to enjoy some of that music very much, but when he examined it spiritually, he had to let it go."

"Really? Is it that bad?" the younger man wondered aloud.

"The next time you're listening to it, step into the spiritual realm and you'll see it for what it is. My suggestion is to find some new music by Christian artists to listen to. I know there are many making music that is honouring to the Lord and still very enjoyable."

"Okay." He wasn't happy to hear that, but he was also curious to discover what the older man was talking about.

"Supper is on the table. Wash your hands and come eat," the lady of the house firmly yet politely instructed the two men. The smell of a fresh cooked meal was intoxicating and reminded Ben of Nancy's cooking. He caught his breath for a moment, pausing mid-step to keep his emotions in check, then carried on.

After washing up, they sat in a small dining room at a table that fit in the room with just enough space around it for seating. Harold gave thanks, and Ben surveyed the meal before him. In a glass casserole dish was a deep bed of browned and seasoned rice mixed with small slices of carrots, topped with de-boned pork chops. The savoury aroma was overwhelming, and he quickly but respectfully portioned out some of the meal on his plate.

"Have you been reading?" Harold asked as they ate.

"Yes, I read on my breaks at work and at home as well. I've read about ten chapters so far."

"A good practice is to pray and ask for the Holy Spirit's guidance before reading. After all, He is the one who wrote it."

"Does it say that somewhere in the Bible?"

"Second Timothy 3:16 says, '*All scripture is given by inspiration of God, and is profitable for doctrine, for reproof, for correction, for instruction in righteousness.*'"

"I'll look that up later."

They continued to chat while they consumed the remainder of food from their plates.

After a ten-minute break to allow the main course to settle, Doreen asked, "Who's ready for some orange stuff?"

"Orange stuff" was a dessert that, as the name indicated, simply looked like orange-coloured … stuff. If Ben had to describe it more clearly, he would say it looked like pale gelatin with pieces of mandarin oranges mixed in. It was delicious.

After the meal, they moved into the small but cozy living area. It was decorated in an older fashion and was nicely furnished and finished yet not expensively so.

Harold suggested they pray, and Doreen put a light cloth covering on her head, something Ben remembered Nancy doing. After the "Amen," he looked at the two with him and once again saw them as soldiers, both in their respective armour. He was a little surprised at this little old lady also being a soldier of light, and indicated so.

"I guess all who become believers in Christ are soldiers in His army?"

"Yes, Ben, every one of us has a part in furthering the gospel and is equipped for that very task," Doreen responded. "I fight through prayer mostly. I'm what we call a prayer warrior."

"Okay, are there other types of warriors besides soldiers and prayer warriors?" Ben found it interesting that there were other types of fighters in this spiritual war.

"Oh yes, the body of Christ has many parts, as it says in 1 Corinthians 12:12–27. Some are leaders of the church, such as elders, bishops, deacons, etc. Others do other things like street preaching, helping the homeless by donations and assisting with soup kitchens, things like that. There are also many other parts of the body of Christ that all work together to push back the darkness so that others may join the family."

This was all very interesting, but Ben wanted to discuss his attack from the darkness.   "I had something happen while I was reading yesterday, something I didn't think would happen anymore."

"You had an attack from the darkness, right?"

"Yes, I thought the darkness was a part of my past, something I wouldn't have to deal with anymore!"

A light chuckle from Harold. Ben was getting used to that.

"Not even close, young soldier, not even close. You're now in the fight and Satan, his demons, sin, and the world will fight against you."

Ben was shocked at this and his expression must have shown this.

"Don't be afraid, you have everything you need to fight against these spiritual enemies," Harold encouraged him.

"And don't forget that part of James 4:7, '*Resist the devil, and he will flee from you*,'" Doreen added.

This actually helped, and Ben recounted the attack he had experienced in full, ending with him verbally saying, "Go away!"

"You resisted and he left, you see?" Ben nodded. "But I want you to realize this was a very minor attack, and not by Satan; this was a very minor demon."

Another surprised look from Ben showed that this wasn't the news he was expecting or wanted.

"No, no, don't give in to fear. Second Timothy 1:7 says, '*For God hath not given us the spirit of fear; but of power, and of love, and of a sound mind*.'" Harold quickly tried to settle his worries. As he was trying to calm the younger man, the front door opened, and a man close to Ben's age walked in.

"Hi, Grandma and Grandpa, sorry I'm late."

"That's okay, Grandson. How was the outreach?"

"A lot of talk, no new believers," Dave dejectedly replied.

"Sorry to hear that," Harold said and then turned toward Ben. "Meet Ben. He's a new soldier in the Army of God."

"Good to meet you, Ben. I'm Dave." An outstretched hand and a welcoming smile came Ben's way. He accepted the greeting and shook hands with the newcomer.

"Hi, Dave, I'm new to this whole thing, but I'm eager to learn."

"That's great. Grandpa thought we should talk, and I'm ready to help with any questions you may have."

They talked for a couple of hours and exchanged cell phone numbers, with Dave telling Ben that he could call anytime. At the end of night, Ben went home feeling greatly encouraged and was even more eager to explore his newfound faith in Christ.

EİGHT

Saturday morning Ben slept in for the first time in a very long time. He felt he must have needed it due to all the stress he'd been under, not to mention the drinking he'd done since Nancy had died. Feeling rejuvenated, he again put on his classic rock and started listening to it as he went about cleaning up some small areas of his home. Remembering Harold's advice on the music, he stepped into the spiritual view and took a look around his living area. What he saw surprised and intrigued him.

Floating through the air seemed to be shimmering smoke, which wafted out of the stereo speakers and drifted about his home! The smoke seemed to have a metallic quality to it, glinting at different angles and seeming to amplify the effect of the music and lyrics. Concentrating hard, Ben examined the smoke and was able to see past the outer metallic shell of it, observing that the inner content was a deep, sooty black core. He tried to step back out of the spiritual realm but found he was stuck in it, and that's when he remembered about eating and drinking. He could still see his apartment, so he stepped into the kitchen and made a coffee while "locked" in spirit mode. As the smell of the freshly brewed coffee hit his nostrils, he quickly snapped back into the physical realm. Breathing a little heavily, Ben took a sip of the brew and carefully considered what he had just witnessed.

The music seemed to be somehow reflecting like light, but it wasn't the same light that came from the Word of God. It was a lesser light, something that wasn't of God but was trying to look like it was. Ben began to understand that the music had the ability to fool people into thinking it was something good, but it was actually a deceptive thing. He was rather disappointed with this revelation because he really loved the music—he always had, from as young as he could remember. The idea of leaving his favourite music behind was a very hard thing to imagine. He felt quite sad at this proposition, but somehow he knew it was the prodding of the Holy Spirit for him to do so. Bowing his head, Ben felt the need to pray.

"Lord Jesus, I feel the Holy Spirit is telling me to let go of this music. You know how much I've enjoyed these songs for so many years, Lord. This is something that I find very, very difficult to do, but I want to honour you, so I ask for your help with this commandment, please. In your holy name. Amen."

After praying, he felt a little better, and he suddenly remembered that his wife had programmed a Christian station on their stereo. He began randomly pressing the buttons. A few presets later, he found the station she used to listen to and just let it play. The music wasn't anything he recognized, but some of it was okay, and a few songs he actually found himself enjoying.

He stepped into the spiritual view, and what he saw now was very different from what he had witnessed with the old music. Wafting from the speakers this time were streams of light floating in the air like a warm, pleasant breeze! The light in these streams was the same as what he saw when he was reading the Word of God, so he knew this was a much better choice for listening to.

The rest of the day went without incident, and Ben went to bed early to prepare for the next day's church service. He fell into a deep sleep, and a few hours later was plunged into a horrifying nightmare!

In the dream, Ben was facing a terrifying sight. A large, smoky-black figure was standing before him. It was dressed in a full set of armour, which seemed almost to be a part of its own body. A large horned helmet adorned its head, and it had a gigantic, demonic sword in its right hand. A hand-held crossbow loaded with fiery darts in its left hand completed its arsenal. Ben was standing before this being clothed in his own spiritual armour, and they were locked in heavy combat!

The demon was mocking him. It chuckled and said, "Do you think you can just walk away from us? We'll never let you go!"

A fiery dart shot from the crossbow as it attempted to discourage him, and Ben felt its heat as the sharpness of it grazed his face, drawing blood. Remembering a verse from scripture, Ben replied while swinging his own weapon, "*If the Son therefore shall make you free, ye shall be free indeed*" (John 8:36).

A strong blow knocked the crossbow out of the demon's hand, and Ben heard it grunt in pain. The demon reacted quicker than he could have imagined and swung the huge sword. Ben just had time to lift his shield to block the blow, but it was swung with such force that he was knocked off of his feet! Crashing to the floor on his back, Ben had the wind knocked out of him but was able to keep the shield above him, blocking the pummeling of his opponent's weapon.

He cried out in desperation. "Lord Jesus, please help me!"

A large blinding flash of light moments later, and an angel stood between him and the demon! Getting to his feet while the angel kept the demon's attention, Ben readied himself and jumped back into the fray. Over the next few minutes, the angel and Ben fought side by side, trading blows with the demon until it finally fled while screaming profanities at the two of them. Exhausted, Ben sat on the edge of his bed, now realizing he was actually awake and this had been a very real battle! The angel stood before him, shining in all of its God-given brilliance.

"Well done, human. You have much to learn, but this was no easy foe. The enemy feels the need to keep you from growing in your faith because he fears what you will do for the Lord."

Ben was stunned. Well done? He'd been knocked down by his enemy and would have been slaughtered if not for this unexpected heavenly ally.

"I feel like I failed in this battle. How is it you tell me well done?" he asked incredulously.

"You cried out for help when you were in dire need. You didn't ask before you needed it, but you didn't hold back from asking either when you did, and you also re-entered the battle when you could. Many warriors have great trouble with these parts of the battle. They're too afraid to engage the enemy and therefore ask for help before they actually need it. Others, due to pride, never ask for help in battle, even when they're at their most desperate, so they are seriously injured spiritually. The remainder stop fighting when we come to help, so they don't learn how to fight against these enemies on their own."

"Who are you?" Ben wanted to know.

"I'm one of your guardians, and whenever you're in great need, I will assist when you call for me. My name is Nathaniel. I must leave now, as another needs me." With that statement, the brilliant being vanished in a flash of light!

Ben was stunned at what he had just experienced. He'd fought a demon and met an angel! The whole situation was overwhelming, and he remembered that Dave had said he could call anytime, so he quickly dialed the number.

"Hello?" a very sleepy Dave answered.

"Dave, I just fought a demon and met an angel!"

Silence followed for a few seconds, and then Dave excitedly said, "Okay, oh wow, that's so cool! Let's meet at Murphy's and talk about this. I'll be there in about fifteen minutes. Sound good?"

"Yeah, okay, I'll see you then!"

Ben got himself dressed and quickly drove to Murphy's. He grabbed a booth and ordered coffee and donuts for both of them.

Dave walked in a few minutes later to find the refreshments waiting. He looked a bit haggard but smiled at Ben and said, "So what happened? You look a bit frazzled."

Ben recounted the entire experience from the start in the dream to the final moment when Nathaniel had vanished. When he finished, he saw that Dave had fully awoken and was smiling hugely at him.

"That's so cool!"

"It was scary, I gotta tell you!"

"Yeah, but the angel coming to help you on your first major battle is very encouraging!" Dave was exultant!

"This isn't common?" Ben was confused. He thought this would have been something every soldier experienced.

"No, not at all. A lot of soldiers go through many battles without getting the divine assistance you got tonight."

Ben then remembered what Nathaniel told him about asking for help at the correct time, and he reiterated that part of the experience to Dave.

"Yes, I see that you have a good understanding of when to call out for help, but there's something more going on here." He paused in thought and then his eyes lit up with revelation. "You must have someone in your circle of influence that can be used of the Lord in a mighty way if they become a believer, or maybe someone you encourage will go on to do great things spiritually!"

"What is my circle of influence?" Ben had never heard this term before.

"It's the people you come into contact with. Some of them have no interaction with any other believers in Christ. For some of them, you're the only one who can show them Jesus and His love for them." Ben saw how this made sense, and he began to mentally go through the people he came into contact with.

"Don't try to figure out who it is." Dave interrupted his thoughts. "You'll only create a problem for yourself and maybe damage the influence you have on this person."

"Really?" Ben asked aloud.

"For sure. Read the story of the leper cleansed by Jesus in Mark 1:40–45. The man was told by the Lord to not tell anyone about it, but he went and told everyone he saw. The last verse says that because of this, Jesus could no more openly enter that city, and the people had to come out to the desert to come to Him."

They talked for a few minutes more, and Dave then yawned and looked at his watch. "Oh man, it's three in the morning. We need to get some sleep so we can get to the service tomorrow. It is Sunday morning, after all."

"Oh man, with all of this excitement, I forgot what day it was!"

They parted ways, and the rest of the night went without further incident.

ΠİΠΕ

B en arose early for the Sunday morning service. After going through his closet, he knew he needed to get some better clothes for church services, but for now he dressed in the best he had. Arriving with ten minutes to spare, he found Harold and Doreen already there, sitting in their favourite pew. He gave a quiet greeting and sat next to them, glancing around the room.

Harmony Christian Fellowship was a very nice church building and felt very welcoming. Soon the singing began, and as he joined in, Ben felt himself slip easily into the spiritual realm. As he viewed the worship leaders on stage, he saw they were all fully clad in the armour of God and glowing brightly. A few songs later, the announcements were read and a prayer was used to open the sermon. Ben followed in his own Bible as the speaker led them through the sermon, and he enjoyed it greatly. As they were singing the final hymn, Ben looked around the auditorium at the rest of the congregation. What he saw surprised him very much.

Many of the members were bright and fully armour-clad, but a lot of them weren't. Several were fully clad in spiritual armour, but the glow coming from them was much less than from others. Some were very dimly lit, their armour much duller than his, while others seemed to have no light in them at all. The armour they wore was heavily tarnished and had chips and cracks and even chunks missing! He also noticed those in attendance who had no armour at all. He knew these were those who hadn't chosen to follow Jesus, and they had various clouds of darkness clinging to them. The most surprising thing he saw were the believers who, in various condition of armour, had some darkness on them. It was in front of the eyes of some and over the ears of others, but some also had more of it covering a larger part of their bodies! After the closing prayer, he turned to Harold and found the older man looking at him.

"I know," was all he said. "Come over for lunch and we'll talk."

Ben nodded his assent. After a few greetings and acknowledgements, they went to their respective vehicles and drove to the Ontagers' home. After another wonderful meal, finished off with the famous orange stuff, they sat down in the living room. Harold gave Ben a knowing look.

"You looked over the congregation, didn't you?"

"Yeah. I don't understand what I saw, all of those members in various states of armour and the ones with the darkness on them. What does all of that mean? How can they have darkness on them and their armour be in such a sad state?" Ben was very confused about all of it.

"Some Christians don't follow Christ as closely as you and I try to do. Some have forgotten their first love, so they aren't keeping their armour in good condition. There are even those who have taken off their armour or never put all of it on. You see, the apostle Paul instructed us in Ephesians 6:11–17 to '*put on the whole armour of God*.'"

"I did see a couple of people who only had a helmet on. How does that work?"

"Once saved, always saved, I like to say. In John 10:28–30, Jesus said:

> And I give unto them eternal life; and they shall never perish, neither shall any man pluck them out of my hand. My Father, which gave them me, is greater than all; and no man is able to pluck them out of my Father's hand. I and my Father are one.

After Harold recited the passage, he held his left hand cupped and said, "This is Jesus, and we are in His hand." Harold then cupped his right hand and placed it over his left. "This is the Father's hand. We're safe inside the hands of the Father and the Son."

Ben felt very encouraged by this and could see how it made sense. "But what about those who had the darkness on them? How can they be believers yet have darkness on them?"

"These are those who are resisting the Holy Spirit and who have set their minds on earthly things. They're blinded by their own desires, lusting after fleshly things."

"Which scriptures support this?" Ben wanted to learn more of this subject.

"Paul wrote in Ephesians 4:30: '*grieve not the Holy Spirit.*' This would be doing things that are against the Lord's will for us, and I believe this is one way we can stunt our spiritual growth as well. First Thessalonians 5:19 simply states: '*Quench not the Spirit.*'"

"What does 'quench' mean?" He had never heard that word before.

"To quench means to put out, like pouring water on a fire to keep it from getting larger, or to put it out altogether. Some Christians hear the Holy Spirit telling them something that they don't like and they resist or push back against the instruction they have received."

"Okay, I understand. Is there anything else to explain the spiritual condition of those people I saw today?"

"One more scripture I can refer you to is Revelation 2:1–6. This is where John was instructed by Jesus to give instruction to the church of Ephesus. He praises them for the faithfulness they have shown, but in verse 4 he states that they have left their first love. He then admonishes them to repent of this."

Ben wrote down the references and assured Harold that he would read them later and study the information contained therein. He took his leave of them, thanking them for their hospitality, and drove back to his home. None of them noticed the dark shadows hiding nearby that had listened in on their conversation.

ᵗＥП

The next two weeks went without incident or spiritual attack. Ben studied many scriptures and attended Bible study meetings, prayer meetings, and Sunday services. He had feelings of such joy during those moments that he almost couldn't believe it.

The third week was not so full of joy.

First of all, Harold, Doreen, and Dave were away at a spiritual retreat for the week, so he didn't have his spiritual support network. Then the real problems began.

It started at work. Kranti was with him on a coffee break, and what happened disturbed Ben to his core.

"Hey, you should see this video. This kid was so stupid."

Ben knew there was likely something about the video that he wouldn't like, but he foolishly leaned over to view the other man's phone. The video was of a group of Asian teens diving off some cliffs into small pools of water. One particular boy jumped from about thirty feet up but missed the pool, landing on his face! They rolled him over, and his face was so horrifyingly injured that Ben knew he likely was dead or soon would be.

"Don't show me things like that!" He was outraged, and it showed.

"It's just news from Asia," Kranti retorted.

"I don't want to see it!" Ben again told him and angrily walked away while Kranti muttered something offensive.

The next night, Ben was careful to avoid Kranti, and he worked absentmindedly unloading the trailer he had been assigned. After finishing the trailer, he forgot to put his gloves on while putting the square-shaped load bar back into the trailer. As he slid his hand along the load bar to balance it better, a sudden very sharp pain pierced his palm, and he dropped the load bar, swearing from the agony. Clutching his hand, he saw a large gash across his palm that was bleeding very quickly, and he knew he needed medical attention.

He called out for help, and another co-worker came to see what was going on and then called for First Aid. Cleaning the wound in the First Aid room, the attendant determined that he would need stitches and called the cab for him. Returning to work hours later, Ben filled out the appropriate paperwork, gave an account of what had happened, and went home to rest and begin recovering from his injury.

The doctor had recommended that he take the rest of the week to recover and then return to work the following Monday. Ben wasn't happy with losing two days' pay, but he had no choice in the matter, so he agreed to this. It was discovered that the load bar had been damaged, producing a sharp spur on the one cornered edge. Ben berated himself for being so distracted that he forgot his gloves, which would have prevented this injury.

The darkness chuckled.

Continuing in the bad mood of the previous two days, Ben arose Wednesday morning and put some classic rock on, ignoring the previous warnings resonating in his head. If he had stepped into the spiritual realm, he would have seen several dark entities closing in on him, but he was so absorbed with his physical problems that he didn't take the time to do so. He felt that the music was improving his mood, but it was in fact lessening the brightness of his spiritual glow, allowing the darkness and the beings contained therein to get much closer to him. This made them and the rest of the darkness very, very happy.

ELEVEN

He slept and dreamt—not of demons and terrors, but of a woman. She was someone he knew, someone he had spent time with, been comforted by, and even had a physical relationship with.

It was in the latter context that the dream was focused.

Ben was with Kathy in the dream. She was very attractive and two years younger than him. Things were getting very heated up when Ben began to realize that he was dreaming and that it was becoming very sinful. He tried to shift into the spiritual realm but found he had great difficulty doing so, and he could not maintain it. Feeling greatly despondent about this, he reminded himself that the dream was wrong, although it was sinfully appealing. After struggling severely and crying out to the Lord for help, he awoke in a great sweat, and it took him a few minutes to realize that he was no longer asleep.

"What on earth?" he questioned aloud. He knew the enemy was attacking him, and he tried to pray, but it came out weak and was very short.

The darkness was pleased.

Clearing the cobwebs from his mind, he turned off his alarm when it sounded and thought about Kathy. He had first gotten involved with her in high school. They'd dated for two years and were almost inseparable, but rumours of a party she attended and her supposed infidelity at this party caused them to break up. A few months later, he met Nancy and never looked back.

Until Nancy died.

Kathy had comforted him, still having strong feelings for him and having heard of his loss, and during those days they began a casual relationship again. Ben suddenly realized he hadn't seen Kathy in a few weeks, not since the night he tried to commit suicide, and he felt he should explain to her what had happened to him. He dialed her number but only got her voicemail, so he left a message apologizing for being silent for so long and asking her to call him. Ben decided to keep busy and went to do a few small repairs on the truck that he had been putting off.

A couple of hours later, he was pleased with the results of the repairs and was just putting his tools away when a car pulled into his driveway and a familiar face poked out the driver's window.

Kathy.

"Hey, stranger!"

She was smiling and seemed to be happy but concerned as she exited the vehicle. Striding up the driveway, she wasn't her usual bubbly self, exclaiming, "It's about time you called, Ben. What happened?"

"Wait, I need to get washed up. I'm a little grubby here." He held out his grease-covered hands. "Could you get the door please?"

She complied with his request, and he got washed up in the small bathroom while she waited.

"I'm so sorry, Kath. I've had a life changing experience, but I didn't mean to forget about you."

"I was so worried about you. I even left you a few voicemails!"

"I know. I'm sorry. Please let me tell you what happened." She sat down and waited for his explanation, and he told her everything. She looked at him afterwards with a mix of emotions, and it was evident from the look on her face that she had a lot of questions.

"So what does that mean for us? Are you expecting me to just become a Christian now as well?"

"I'm hoping you will, but it's your choice of course."

She cuddled up to him on the couch suddenly and said, "I was so happy that you called. I was hoping we could make up for lost time." She gave him a loving squeeze and kissed him passionately. He responded in kind initially but quickly pulled away.

"No, Kathy, I can't just keep sinning against Jesus this way. It's also not respecting you to do this."

"What?" It was clear that she didn't understand at all. "How is loving me not respecting me? Ben, I really don't get you right now!" With that she got up and stormed out of the house. He followed, trying to convince her to stay and hear him out, but she got in her car and raced out of sight.

TWELVE

S aturday morning came and Ben awoke with Kathy on his mind.

He hadn't slept well and it showed. He looked haggard in the mirror and felt just as rough. He had tried to call her but she wasn't answering the phone, and this only added to his less than stellar mood. Suddenly the phone rang and he quickly grabbed it.

"Kathy?"

"No, sorry, didn't mean to disappoint."

Harold.

"Oh, hey, Harold, I've had a rough week … it's a long story."

"Well, Doreen wanted me to invite you for breakfast at our place. Why don't you come on over and tell us about it?"

Ben knew this was what he really had been missing this week—good Christian fellowship. He was reluctant to accept this invitation and dump his weekly problems on them, but he knew he needed the spiritual support after the week he'd had, so he drove to the now familiar bungalow.

Harold took one look at him and said, "I can see you meant it when you said you'd had a rough week." Ben only nodded.

Doreen, having heard Harold's statement, came into the living room, took one look at Ben, and said, "Let's have breakfast and then you can tell us what has happened."

She was already treating him like a son, such was her nature, and Ben felt some stress release from him just from her kind tone. They enjoyed bacon, eggs, toast, and coffee. Afterwards, they moved to the living room to relax and discuss the week's events.

Ben relayed everything in order, beginning with Kranti's video sharing that had so greatly disturbed him.

"Seems like this kind of media is just considered to be news in that part of the world," Harold stated, but he could see how much it troubled Ben, and he continued. "I know it's disgusting to us, but you're going to have to try to avoid watching any more videos that he tries to share with you."

"Easier said than done," Ben said flatly. "You don't realize how pushy he is. There are no personal boundaries with him, none at all!" He was starting to get angry, which happened almost every time when he talked about Kranti. The man made him angry.

"Prayer first, always prayer first when you're concerned about a situation."

"I know. I wasn't expecting this, so I wasn't praying about it, but maybe I should have prayed anyway, because I know his character." It was obvious that Ben felt disappointed with himself.

Harold smiled. "I think you just had an epiphany of sorts. Yes, knowing a person or enough of a situation beforehand means we should pray before entering the situation or engaging that person."

Doreen looked at him and added, "We'll pray for him and for you in this situation." Then she looked concerned and, pointing at his bandaged hand, said, "What happened there? Please tell me you didn't get into a round of fisticuffs with this man!"

Ben actually laughed lightly at this, and it eased some tension about Kranti.

"No, no, we didn't fight. This was an accident." With that, he relayed the details of the injury and the advised time off, which led him to Kathy. He wasn't sure how to tell them about the dream, which was more raunchy than he felt comfortable sharing with them, but he felt the spiritual side of that was important.

"The part of this week that bothers me the most is … Kathy."

Harold and Doreen looked at each other with a knowing look that said they seemed to be suspecting something of this nature.

"Who's Kathy?" A simple question without a simple answer, so Ben started at high school and recounted his history with Kathy, ending with her driving off the previous day.

"I just wanted to tell her about what I've found in Jesus and somehow show her that she needs to choose Him for herself." He appeared more discouraged than when he had first arrived, and Doreen was the first to speak.

"We'll pray for her. The Lord will speak to her in His time and way, you'll see."

Ben took as much encouragement from this as he could.

THIRTEEN

en's hand healed well, and he was back to work the following week. Kranti made comments about it, some seemingly caring and some definitely not. Over the next few months, Ben faced several challenges from the dark forces, from within himself, and from Kranti as well. He found himself questioning spiritual matters, even his own salvation, yet he knew the truth. So why was he fighting within himself on these matters? He knew he had to have some hard conversations with Harold, which he wasn't looking forward to, but he was determined to seek the answers.

He had a few spiritual battles as well with various types of dark beings. Some of these were fairly easy to defeat, but there were also a couple that were tough, and he even had another one that Nathaniel assisted with again. He bore some spiritual scars from the more major battles, and he noticed some markings on his armour as well, but his shield was growing larger, which encouraged him.

Then came a day when Kranti showed him another horrifying video of news from somewhere in Asia. It was a graphic report of someone dying, and Ben again told him he didn't want to see that. Kranti didn't understand, and as Ben walked away, he heard the accusations of weakness coming from the other man. He ignored the nasty comments and began to pray, asking for the Lord's help. He found himself praying a lot more now than when he first became a Christian. He had joined a Bible study group at Harmony that met Friday evenings, and he was enjoying getting together with other Christians.

Kathy finally called him and they talked in depth about his faith in Jesus, and she even admitted that he had changed very much for the better. She did attend the service on Sundays a few times but so far hadn't made a choice to trust Jesus. Doreen had made a friend of her though, and Ben observed that the younger woman seemed to very much enjoy the elder's company. He was hopeful that Doreen could help Kathy find Christ, because he was also beginning to realize that he did care for her. He knew from scripture that they couldn't date because they would be unequally yoked, so he waited and let the Lord have His time with Kathy.

Another event that he started to attend was the Saturday night outreaches run by Dave and the outreach group from Harmony. Dave kept encouraging him to come to these, and Ben had a feeling there was more to it, but nothing specific was mentioned.

A few weeks later on a beautiful Saturday, Kathy called him and told him that she had accepted Jesus as her Lord and Saviour! Ben was ecstatic as he listened to her spill out everything she had experienced so far as a new believer. They had dinner with Harold and Doreen one night, and there were some new realizations for both, spiritually and emotionally. Kathy was born spiritually as a support warrior. This was someone who quite often was with the warrior of light during their battles and prayed while the fight was going on in order to assist the warrior. Harold and Doreen were both overjoyed that this was her spiritual placement in the body of Christ, as they said there was a lack in this area at Harmony right now. As they were leaving the couple's home, Ben and Kathy looked at each other and knew they both had strong feelings for one another.

"I think we should pray about this first, before we decide to date even," Kathy suggested, and Ben agreed. They sat in his truck and asked Jesus for His answer about them becoming a couple and then went their separate ways, agreeing to pray on their own about it too.

As he watched her go, Ben thought that she had never looked more beautiful.

FOURTEEN

They talked a lot about their feelings for each other over the next few weeks. Harold and Doreen had obviously noticed, and Harold had given Ben the advice to pray first. Both Ben and Kathy had done so, and they agreed that for now, both of them were in need of spiritual growth before they started to actually date. They also agreed that seeing each other at the various functions run by the church would allow them to spend time together. Life for Ben was far happier than he could have imagined such a short time ago. He was blissfully happy in Christ and saw the potential for a new serious relationship with Kathy that he was excited about.

The darkness was growing angry.

About a month later, Ben finally had the last straw he could take from Kranti, as he showed him yet another video that disgusted him. Ben was so distraught over what he had seen in this video that he couldn't finish his shift. The scene just kept playing over and over in his head, and he almost got physically ill from it. The next day at work, Ben felt that he had to report this to the human resource department. He sat upstairs with the lady from that part of the company for about an hour, giving his account of the things Kranti had both said and done toward him and others. After providing a written statement, he was advised to "just try to stay away from him." *Easier said than done*, he thought. Kranti was the type of guy to purposely seek out a person and then chew them out for whatever he felt they needed it for. The following day they both received letters from the HR department stating that they were involved in an investigation.

Kranti was furious, and it was very obvious that he was also pretty worried about the repercussions from this. He began to desperately try to find out who had done this. He even talked with Ben about it, never suspecting that it was him. His number one suspect was Sammy, a guy who had never gotten along with Kranti. There had been some seriously bad incidents between the two of them, but as yet nothing that either could be fired for.

As another month passed, Kranti used every resource he could to discover who the "rat" was who had run to HR. Ben didn't know how it happened or who had pointed Kranti in his direction, but it became clear that he had a very good idea that Ben was to blame.

Kranti started making more comments about there being too many rats in the warehouse whenever he was close enough for Ben to hear him. Ben had talked to Harold about this, and while the older man was empathetic toward what he was being put through, he also suggested that going to HR might not have been the best choice.

"I didn't have a choice," Ben told him.

"We always have a choice, but it doesn't mean we will like what those choices are."

Ben was very frustrated with that comment, although he recognized the truth of it.

FIFTEEN

D ave closed the outreach service in prayer and called Ben over to him.

"Hey, I really appreciate all of the help tonight."

"No problem. I think we're making a real difference here."

"We are, and I wanted to make a suggestion to you, a request actually."

"Oh?" Ben's curiosity was up.

"I think we're ready to expand our efforts, and I'd like for you to help with that."

"Cool, what did you have in mind?"

"I've talked with the elders at Harmony, and they agree that a second site for outreach services is possible. I'd like you to lead that site."

Ben was astounded. He knew that he had grown spiritually, but he wasn't sure that he was ready for such an important project! Dave saw the apprehension on his face.

"Don't make a decision right now. We won't be ready to start this for a couple more weeks. Just pray about it and wait for the Lord's answer." He nodded and bid farewell to his friend and brother in the Lord.

• • •

Ben was sitting on his couch listening for an answer. He had just poured his heart out to Jesus in prayer. He asked about Kathy and the new outreach position that Dave had offered him. He even asked about the horrible situation with Kranti. He wasn't certain about any of these things, and what surprised him was that he actually found himself weeping while in prayer. The stresses of it all must have been heavier on him than he realized.

As he contemplated all of these questions, suddenly an angel appeared before him! Ben instinctively drew back from this shining being before him.

"Be not afraid," the celestial being said in a powerful voice. "I was sent to you with a message."

This piqued Ben's curiosity. "Okay, what's the message?"

"You're doing enough; this new outreach can be handled by another."

Not what he had expected.

"Really? I thought the Lord wanted more from me. I thought I was being trained for something bigger."

Something strange showed on the angel's face when Ben mentioned the Lord. The visitor continued. "In time you will do more, much more than you are now, but the strains on you are becoming too much."

Seemed to fit with the stresses he had just realized, Ben thought, yet somehow he wasn't certain of this message. He took a closer look at this angel before him and noticed that the glow from him was different than the previous angels he'd encountered. He couldn't explain it, but the impressive stature of this spiritual being caused him to stop questioning things.

"Okay, thanks," was all that he could muster. With that confirmation of acceptance, the angel vanished.

SIXTEEN

B en had told Dave he wasn't sure about taking on that new ministry. Dave said he understood, but Ben felt the disappointment from the other man.

"Why do you feel this way about it?" Dave asked.

Ben then relayed his visit from the heavenly being and what he had been told. A knowing glance between Harold and Dave told Ben that there was something they were aware of that he wasn't.

"What is it?"

Harold spoke first. "What did this 'angel' look like?" A deep look of concern was on his face.

"He was different from the others that I've met. His brightness was far less intense, and he was very large, much larger than any other celestial being I've seen."

A deep, worried sigh escaped the older man. "I thought so," was all that he said at first, and then he continued. "Satan." As he said the name, he looked into Ben's eyes so that he would know that he was serious. "You've attracted his attention, and now he's trying to keep you from the Lord's work for you."

If Ben thought he was shocked before, it was nothing compared to what he felt in this moment. Doreen reached out to touch his arm. "Get ahold of yourself, son; it happens to every believer."

Another look of surprise caused the lady warrior to continue. "'*Be sober, be vigilant; because your adversary the devil, as a roaring lion, walketh about, seeking whom he may devour*' (1 Peter 5:8). Don't let him."

"Don't let him what?"

"Devour you."

As it sank in, Ben began to feel much relief.

"Let's pray," Harold suggested and led them in prayer for Ben. Afterwards, Ben accepted the position of leading the new outreach site, and then he took his leave of the Ontagers to head home.

SEVENTEEN

W ork had gotten worse. Kranti had been up to his usual spitefulness. This time he'd teamed up with one supervisor to spy on Ben. The only way Ben found out about this was that Sammy had discovered it and relayed the information to him. He was furious over this but remembered what the previous HR report had done, so he didn't file a new report. He did call and speak with Harold and Doreen about it over the phone, and they commended his choice to not go to HR again, though they did recognize how difficult this situation was for him. After a prayer session, he hung up and carried on with his day.

A few weeks later, the supervisor in question was moved to dayshift and no longer presented a problem for him. One day he got a call from Sammy.

"Hey, man, can you give me a ride to work and home? My bike's in the shop. I'll give you gas money."

"Sure, no problem, I can do that."

The night went so well Ben was amazed; even Kranti was unusually pleasant and seemingly happy throughout the shift.

When they punched out in the morning, Ben met up with Sammy and they got into the old pickup for the ride home. They were chatting on the drive home, and at the crest of a hill there was suddenly a vehicle coming straight at them in their lane! The guy had been passing going uphill! Ben tried to steer away from the imminent collision but it was unavoidable. As the two vehicles met, the impact was tremendous and sent the truck careening off of the road and into the ditch. Dirt and debris flew everywhere as the truck plowed and rolled its way through the topsoil, finally coming to rest in a field.

The last thing Ben knew before he passed out was that Sammy was calling his name.

EIGHTEEN

Waking up, the first thing Ben realized was that he was in a hospital bed. The second was the large group of people around the bed—some bowed in prayer, three of four sleeping in chairs, and one who realized that he had awoken.

"Hey, welcome back!" It was Doreen. "We've all been so worried about you." The rest of the group then began offering their greetings and support. Sammy was there too; he appeared to be unhurt from the crash.

"Hey, man, I'm so glad you're awake. I was so afraid after the accident." Tears were apparent in the other man's eyes.

"Thanks, man. Are you hurt?"

Sammy just shook his head. "No, not a scratch. I dunno how." There was bewilderment on his face.

"You know there's a Bible in the glovebox of the truck, right? Maybe that had something to do with it," Ben revealed.

As Sammy realized that he had been sitting on that side of the truck, he stated, "Wow, maybe …"

At this point, Kathy stepped in, and Ben could tell she'd been crying, but she seemed so happy that he had awoken.

"Hi." One tiny word, but it meant so much to him.

"Hi back." With that response, she knew how much he appreciated her.

He had suffered a broken leg, some cracked ribs, severe bruising from the seatbelt, a sprained left wrist, a large gash on his forehead, and various other cuts and bruises. He found out that he had been unconscious for two days. Now that he was awake, the doctor said he would go home after one more day of observation, as long as there were no further concerns.

ПIПETEEП

en's recovery was rough. He couldn't drive, even if he had a vehicle, which he didn't. Kathy had been a huge help, however, driving him wherever he needed to go. During the healing process, he was unable to work, so he spent a lot of time at Harmony and with the Ontagers. He had some good conversations with Harold about spiritual matters. During one such discussion, the older man told him something that he hadn't thought of.

"You know that Satan will kill you if he can, right?"

Ben thought about it a moment then nodded. "Yeah, I guess I should realize that, but why do you say 'if he can?'"

"I refer to the book of Job. Satan argued with God about Job and wanted to do whatever he could to discredit both God and Job. There was a limit, however. God told Satan that he could touch Job but that he must spare his life. So you see, Satan has limitations on what God will allow him to do."

"That's a great thing to know, that God doesn't just let Satan run roughshod all over us." He smiled and added, "What a wonderful Father we have."

"Indeed," agreed Harold.

TWENTY

Two months later, Ben was finally able to return to work. He still had a limp from the broken leg and couldn't use the forklift. It felt great, however, to be back on the job and out of the house. He didn't get a settlement from the insurance for over a month, but eventually they agreed that he wasn't at fault and paid him for the value of his truck and personal injuries. He had picked up another used truck—not a great one, but definitely better than what he had. Kranti actually greeted him kindly, one of the few times he had ever done so.

"How are you doing? Still in pain?" Genuine concern crossed his face.

"Yeah, some pain, but I'm mostly good," Ben replied with a smile.

"What did I miss?" It was a common question at the warehouse.

"Nothing. Everything is the same as always."

Ben nodded in understanding. Nothing further was said for the shift, and over the next few weeks, things settled into a normal kind of routine. Even in his life outside of work, things were calm. He had expected another attack from the dark beings again, or even Satan himself, but there had been nothing.

The call came on a Saturday afternoon. It was Dave, and he sounded rather distraught.

"Ben, please come to the hospital. Grandpa's asking for you."

Ben knew Harold had not been doing well, so he simply got the room number and quickly drove to the hospital. When he got to the correct room, he saw Doreen with Dave on one side of her, and Kathy on the other. Many close family members of the Ontagers were gathered around the bed as well. In the bed was Harold, and he didn't look good, not good at all.

"Hi, Harold," Ben said to Harold's wave over.

"Hello, Ben." A very tired sounding voice escaped the old man. "I wanted to give you one more piece of advice before I go to be with the Lord." Ben's face gave away his feelings. "It's going to happen, so don't be sad. I'm finally going to meet Him face to face." A beaming, calm smile filled his face. "I know you've been careful about taking your time with Kathy, but I believe you've both been patient enough." Ben turned to see Kathy standing beside him. Harold motioned for them to reach a hand out to him. He grasped each of their left hands in both of his and said, "I give my blessing to you both to marry and live in love to the Lord and each other for the rest of your days." Having said this, he became limp and the heart monitor flatlined.

TWENTY-ONE

Harold's funeral was both a happy and sad affair. Ben wept openly for the man he had known for only about a year and a half. Kathy and he held hands. Having taken Harold's advice, they were now dating. Both of them were deliriously happy in their relationship and had plans to marry in six months. Ben looked at Harold in the casket and switched to the spiritual view to see the old soldier laid to rest in his armour, holding the sword of the Spirit on top of him. The hilt was just below his chin, and the tip between his knees. He never looked more magnificent.

Saturday's outreach was in full swing with Ben at the helm. Dave was there in a supporting role, as was Kathy. Ben was talking about Harold and how the old man had led him to the Lord. The group that had gathered seemed to be affected by the tale, and many put their hands up when the altar call was made. As they were getting ready to start packing things up, a very loud, belligerent voice boomed out.

"Don't listen to it! It's all lies!"

Kranti.

This was something Ben had not expected and really didn't want. He knew he had to go about this very carefully, and he focused intently on the spiritual side of things. What he saw scared him to his core.

Dave and Kathy had stepped up behind him, and Ben motioned for them to stay back. Kranti was obviously very drunk and stepped forward to meet Ben.

"This is the big preacher man now, huh?" It was a very mocking tone.

"Hello, Kranti." Ben tried to keep things calm, but he knew the myriad of demons surrounding Kranti wouldn't allow that for long.

He had his sword in his hand, and his shield was ready as the smaller demons were sent forward. A quick back and forth slash easily dispatched the first wave. Larger dark beings began to move toward Ben as he tried to reason with Kranti.

"Did you hear the message?"

"Yeah, I heard what you said about the old man. He sounds like he was nice." Ben blocked a swing from one demon with his shield and took out the other one with his sword. Then Kranti began a tirade against Jesus, and as he did, more larger demons joined the fray just as Ben dispatched the second medium-sized demon.

At this point, he heard Dave and Kathy calling for help from their angelic allies. In a flash of light, three angels landed next to Ben and began quickly to defeat even the largest of this wave of demons. He addressed Kranti again.

"Jesus changed my life, Kranti, and He can change yours too!" Ben could see a tiny sliver of light beginning to crack the dark shield around Kranti. It was barely visible through the heavy cloud surrounding him. A look in his coworker's eyes told him that he wanted to believe. The mass of demons surrounding him had shrunk greatly, and Ben felt hope rising within him. A sudden flash of light mixed with black smoke rocked the area surrounding the drunk man, and with a great crash the largest demon Ben had ever seen landed behind Kranti and laughed.

Satan.

He laid his hands on Kranti's shoulders, and Ben could see the darkness like thick clouds completely envelope the man. A myriad of fiery darts came shooting at them from Satan, and it was difficult to block them all. The angels were still fighting off the remaining minions of Satan, so Ben and his companions focused on the devil himself. They were using every scripture they knew to fend him off.

"Resist the devil and he shall flee from thee!" Kathy swung her sword, landing a glancing blow on the devil's left arm. It seemed to do little harm and only brought further mockery from their enemy.

"You can't beat me! I'm more powerful than all of you combined!" their enemy screamed at them. The angels responded to this by shining more brightly than they thought possible. This increased brightness pushed back the dark clouds, allowing them to see their target more clearly. However, the powerful influence of their adversary was working on the man they were trying to help.

"You reported me to HR for showing you some videos!" Kranti screamed at Ben; he was furious again.

Ben, Dave, and Kathy had thrown all the scriptures they knew at Satan, and they were becoming desperate. Ben had been praying throughout the battle, and a scripture he had forgotten came to mind. As Satan moved his left arm to embrace Kranti and placed his hand over the man's heart, long, sharp claws seemed to sink into the mortal's flesh.

"I'll kill him before I let him go," Satan threatened, and Ben knew it was time to use the only scripture he had left. He shouted it out loudly.

"*The Lord rebuke thee*!" As he yelled this, he drove his sword straight into the back of Satan's hand and directly into Kranti's heart!

Satan screamed, whether in fear, pain, or frustration Ben didn't know, but the evil spirit let go and vanished in a cloud of blackness.

Seeing their enemy was gone, they looked upon the man who had been under his influence. Kranti slumped to his knees, and Ben met him, crouching beside him as he looked up.

"I need Jesus!" Tears streamed down his face, and Ben put his arm around the shoulders of the desperate man. He began to explain the gospel to him, and a few minutes later, the now sober man looked up at the three warriors standing before him and was stunned at their appearance.

"You all are warriors of God!" he declared.

"So are you now," Dave answered.

Ben nodded.

"Welcome to the family."

EPİLOGUE

CIRCLES OF INFLUENCE

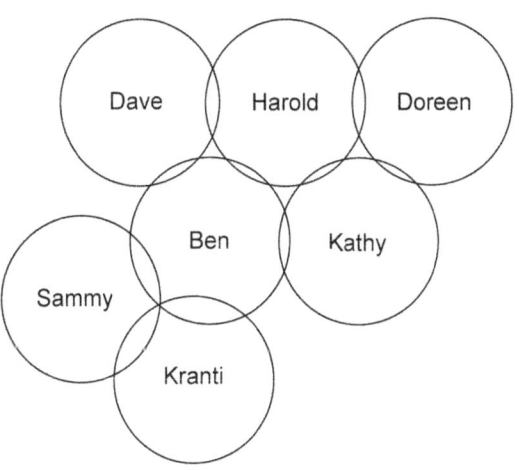

Find out where becoming a Christian takes Kranti
in Robert Dale's next book,

EVANGELIST OF LIGHT.

www.ingramcontent.com/pod-product-compliance
Lightning Source LLC
Chambersburg PA
CBHW051924220626
47052CB00003B/564

* 9 7 8 1 4 8 6 6 2 6 0 0 7 *